BABA means Daddy, MAI means
Mummy, and TSITSI means Grace, in
Shona, one of the many languages
spoken in Zimbabwe.

BLACKIE CHILDREN'S BOOKS

Published by the Penguin Group
Penguin Books Ltd, 27 Wrights Lane, London W8 5TZ, England
Penguin Books Australia Ltd, Ringwood, Victoria, Australia
Penguin Books Canada Ltd, 10 Alcorn Avenue, Toronto, Ontario, Canada M4V 3B2
Penguin Books (NZ) Ltd, 182-190 Wairau Road, Auckland 10, New Zealand

Penguin Books Ltd, Registered Offices: Harmondsworth, Middlesex, England

First published 1993
1 3 5 7 9 10 8 6 4 2
First edition
Text copyright © Janie Hampton 1993
Illustrations copyright © Jenny Bent 1993

A CIP catalogue record for this book is available from the British Library

ISBN 0 216 94019 2

First American edition published in 1993 by

Peter Bedrick Books
2112 Broadway
New York, NY 10023

Library of Congress Cataloging-in-Publication Data
is available for this title
USA ISBN 0 87226 511 0

Made and printed by Imago in Hong Kong

Come home soon, Baba

by Janie Hampton
Illustrated by Jenny Bent

Blackie   Bedrick/Blackie
London   New York

Baba and Blessing stood waiting for the bus.

'Here it comes,' said Baba.

'Please don't go, Baba,' said Blessing.

'I have to go to town to work. There's not enough work for me here,' said Baba.

'While I am away you can help Mai to make bricks. I'll earn money in town to buy a door and some windows and a roof. Then we can build a new room for you and your brothers to sleep in.'

'When will you come back?' asked Blessing.

'I'll come back when the new chicks hatch,' said Baba waving good-bye.

Blessing felt sad. Life was not the same without Baba.

'Now hen,' he said quietly, 'I want you to hatch your eggs double quick time, so that Baba will come home soon.'

The hen looked at Blessing with her beady eye. Nobody told her what to do, not even Blessing. Her job was hatching twelve brown eggs, and she would do it in her own good time.

'Cheer up,' called Mai. 'Come and help us make bricks.'

Blessing followed them down to the stream.

First they dug a hole.

Then they mixed the clay and water together in the hole.

Blessing liked the clay squidging between his toes.

They filled the wooden
moulds with clay.
  Then Mai tipped
the wet bricks onto
the ground.

They sang as they worked and hardly noticed
the time pass.

'That's enough for today,' said Mai. 'It's time
to wash.'

They all jumped into the stream.

Blessing lay in the clear cool water and watched the mud wash off him. It swirled down the stream, like smoke, hiding the coloured stones. He wondered where the water would go. He knew it went into a bigger stream, and then into a river. The river passed through the town and then it reached the sea.

Blessing wished that
he could be the water.
Then he could pass
through the town,
and see his father.

Every day the row of bricks grew longer.

'I think we have enough bricks,' said Blessing. 'We've made hundreds.'

'We still need lots more,' said Tsitsi. 'There's only enough bricks here for a hen house. Do you want to live in a hen house?'

'No,' said Blessing. 'I'm not a hen.'

'If we work hard,' said Mai, 'then the bricks will be ready when Baba comes home.'

Blessing worked very hard. He wanted Baba to come home soon.

'Hurry up, hen.' Blessing scowled at the hen. 'Why haven't your eggs hatched yet?' The hen clucked gently.

Blessing pushed his hand under her. She pecked him hard and he lept back.

'You silly boy,' Mai said. 'The eggs are not ready to hatch yet. You can't hurry these things.'

A few days later Mai said, 'We have
enough bricks. Now we can build the kiln.'

Blessing helped to build the brick kiln. The
bricks were dry and crumbly.

When all the bricks were piled up, they
smeared clay all over the sides. Tsitsi and Mai
lifted Blessing onto their shoulders so that he
could put it on the top.

'This is like painting with your hands,'
said Blessing.

Then they collected a big pile of firewood. Mai pushed the firewood inside the kiln.

'Blessing has worked very hard,' said Mai. 'He may light the fire.'

Blessing lit the dry grass. He blew gently on the small flames and soon they were licking through the inside of the kiln. Then Mai sealed up the kiln with more bricks and clay.

The kiln was so hot that even the ground around it became warm.

They sat in a circle, singing and drinking tea. They kept the fire going all night.

There was a space in the circle where Baba should have been. Blessing thought it looked like a mouth with one of its big teeth missing.

'Baba will be home now we've finished the bricks,' said Blessing. 'That's why I have worked so hard to help you.'

'Be patient, Blessing,' said Mai. 'Some things can be made to happen early, and other things cannot. Time has its own pace. You can't hurry it along.'

When the bricks were cool Blessing helped to break the shell of hard clay around the kiln. The bricks had changed from a dull grey colour to dark orange, like the late afternoon sun.

'These bricks will make a fine new room,' said Mai.

'Let's see if the eggs are hatching,' said Tsitsi.
Tsitsi pushed the hen off the nest. The hen
ran flapping and squawking from the kitchen.

Blessing picked up an egg. It was hot to touch. The shell was smooth and soft. He held it to his face and felt something move against his cheek. He held the egg to his ear.

'Yes!' he whispered. 'It's hatching!'

The egg had a tiny window in the shell. Blessing could see a pink beak and damp, yellow feathers.

This had been the chick's home, so perfectly shaped with no end, no beginning, and no sharp corners. Now the chick had to break the shell into sharp little pieces so that it could start its new life out in the world.

'Go back to your family,' said Tsitsi to the hen. 'They need you to keep them warm.' But the hen just clucked and flapped outside the kitchen.

'She won't go back when one of her eggs is missing,' said Mai. 'Put the egg back now.'

'I'll see you later,' said Blessing as he placed the egg in the nest. The hen ran straight back into the kitchen and sat down on her eggs. She wriggled around, clucked once and was silent.

In the morning there was a chirruping and a squeaking from the nest.

The twelve chicks hid in their mother's warm feathers. Then the hen stepped out of the basket, as if to say, 'I've done my job. Now I deserve a little fresh air.'

The chicks followed after their mother in the sunshine. She clucked proudly. Blessing ran after them, squeaking and chirruping too.

Blessing heard a low rumble in the distance. He saw a small cloud of dust, a long way off. It was the bus! The chicks had hatched, so Baba would be on the bus!

'Baba!' cried Blessing. 'Come and look at the chicks.'

'Look what I have too,' said Baba. 'I worked hard and bought things for the new room.'

'And we worked hard too,' said Blessing. 'We have made all the bricks. I thought you would come home earlier if we finished the bricks quickly. But you didn't come.'

'I said I would come when the chicks hatched. They cannot be hurried like making bricks. Some things you can make happen faster, and some things have their own time.'

Everybody carried something home.
Tomorrow they could start building the
new room for Blessing and his brothers.